· SAVED BY LOVE ·
FROM RESCUE DOG TO ROCK STAR

BY VIRGINIA ULCH, MA

Grizzbear

This book is dedicated to all animals big and small and the humans who love them like family. My wish is that all animals be treated with love and kindness. Thank you to all of the neighborhood friends who indulge Grizzbear and his need to give everyone love.

This book is printed on acid-free paper. Printed in the United States of America

ISBN: 9781707900749

Let me introduce myself. My name is Grizzbear, Golden Retriever Extraordinaire.
Before I was adopted by my family, my name was Prince. I guess that makes me the
dog formerly known as Prince. Lol

1

When I was a pup, I was happy and safe. My mom told me that some people would come one day and take me with them to a home of my own. She told me stories of cuddles, couches, bones, and a life of love. I didn't want to leave my mom but that sounded wonderful too.

When I was old enough, I went to a home with some other dogs. I had high hopes but the people only wanted to breed me and sell our puppies. I guess I was too much for them. I was a happy, hyper guy. I loved to run and play fetch, roll in the mud, play in flower beds, and wrestle with the other dogs. They said I played too rough and separated me from the others. My owner hit me. One day, she hit me really hard on my tail bone and it hurt my back and hips. After that, I couldn't run very well so I didn't play much.

3

They lost interest in me because I wasn't going to make puppies now. I ended up outside on a chain. All I wanted was to love and be loved. I sat out there day after day wishing for them to love me again. I felt like I must be bad and unlovable. Every night, I would watch the other dogs and the humans go in to their warm house to sleep in their comfortable beds. I longed to be in there, too. There would be no soft couches for me. No bones. No snuggles. I lived out in the cold with only a beat up old dog house. I was lonely, in pain, and I was so very sad. I longed for love.

My heart was broken.

One day, some people came and took me away. I was afraid. I didn't understand what was going to happen to me. I got a bath and was brushed out by a very nice lady. They brought me to a store with a lot of strangers and a bunch of other dogs. I noticed I was way bigger than all of the others. I weigh120 pounds so I was twice as big!
The people looked at all of us. A family came in and for some reason, they chose me. I was hopeful. Maybe things would be different. Boy, did I have a lot to learn!

I had not been raised in a house. I didn't have house manners. I made lots of mistakes! I peed everywhere. I ate the remote. I ate a very expensive library book. I was given one of those bones with the knots on the ends. I was so afraid someone would take it, that I swallowed it whole! Ow, that hurt! I kept thinking that now they are going to hit me. I would flinch and close my eyes when they raised their hand toward me. I thought this is the time they are going to make me live outside. There was another dog there. She was super bossy but let me know she had made some of the same mistakes and that I was safe. No one would ever hit me again and they loved me even if I messed up and couldn't play fetch.

Let me introduce you to my crazy family. I have a sister named Zoey. She is a rescue dog too. She is black. Not many people want a black golden retriever so she didn't grow up in a house. She went to live at a kennel as a puppy. When she was adopted, she peed all over the house and was afraid of everything. They should have named her Jealousy. If anyone gets any attention, she has to get in between and push them out of the way. She is a spaz! She gets so excited about walks that she eats the leash! Then, she has to walk way out front and sniff for danger. I am much slower because of my hips but I love my walks. I get so excited that I bunny hop around the room, grab my leash and swing it around. Then, I hand it to Mom.

7

We have 3 cats. There is Munchkin, who was raised with a raccoon, so he has a lot of attitude and fears nothing. If cats wore clothes, he would be wearing a leatherjacket and spikes. When he is mad, he hisses and swats at everyone he sees! He is kind of a bully to everyone but Mom. He is also obsessed with boxes. All the cats like boxes but he gets in them and won't share!

Blackie is a stray that we adopted. He is goofy but he has a good heart. There was another cat with him that was injured. When my dad put food out for them, Blackie always let her eat first. Someone must have dumped them off. Mom and Dad caught her and took her to a vet. The vet found her a home.

Blackie wouldn't let anyone touch him except dad. He wouldn't use his igloo during a really cold spell and had ice on the side of his face. Dad snatched him up and put him in the house. He hid under a shelf for a week. It took him a while to trust but now he is extremely spoiled. He has his tongue sticking out when he is happy- which is always! He is a daddy's boy. His purr is crazy loud!

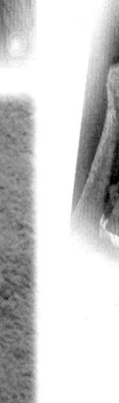

Baby is a bit of a diva and is always posing. We got her when she was just a kitten. I helped raise her and we still spend cuddle time together. At first, I would pick her up and my mouth was so big, my parents thought I was going to eat her. They finally realized that I was only giving her love and taking care of her. She loves to climb up super high and look down on everyone, probably because she thinks she is superior. When she runs, she puts her ears back and looks like she is on a mission. They thought that cats and dogs wouldn't get along but she is like my daughter and we are one big happy family most of the time.

Finally, there is Neal, a Goffin cockatoo. He is a rescue bird. No one is sure what happened to him but he doesn't like to leave his cage. It takes two people to pry him out. He is also a nervous plucker. Most of the time, he is missing feathers. Neal loves music. He is a head banging, foot tapping maniac when he likes a song. He sings, "Yeah Neal". When the song is over, he lifts up his wings and yells, "Yay!" He loves to play peek-a-boo. He waves to visitors and says hi. Boy, does he get mad if people don't say hi back! He tells us, "Night, night Neal," when he wants to go to bed. He gets really pouty if people don't go and sounds like he is crying. He is super funny.

Let me get back to my story. My new family showed me the first compassion I had known. They saw that I was in pain and took me to the vet. I needed surgery to help with my movement. They operated on both knees at the same time so I would only have to go through it once. My dad would pick me up and carry me out to do my business. They stayed home with me and didn't go to work for a few days until they knew I was going to be okay. I have thick, soft beds in my bedroom and the living room to help me be more comfortable. I still have difficulty walking and can't run and play but they do things with me that I can enjoy and accept me as I am.

Sometimes, I can't believe how different things are. From a lonely, cold life to a soft bed, a warm house, being a member of a family, and treats. I will do most anything for treats. Most of all, I am loved. We all got very lucky that these people chose us. Some humans think that we are just animals that don't have feelings but we do. We have different personalities and different likes but we all want to love and be loved. Think of us as kids in fur pajamas. We also all love Christmas!

The only thing I love more than my walks and my treats is being with kids. A child's heart is innocent and loyal much like the heart of a dog. I think that is why I want to connect with children. I want to give them the love I didn't have as a pup and I get love back in return. It is healing for me. When I am really feeling the need for some love, I know I can get to Mom with "the look". It works every time and she gives in. Of course, Ms. Jealousy had to get in on the act when she saw it worked for me!

So how am I a rockstar? Mom likes to walk us different routes to keep it fresh. When I see a person that might need love, I stop and won't move until they come out to see me. Most people will come pet me. Now, the kids and even adults watch for me to come. I hear, "Grizzbear", wherever I go! Sometimes they even leave us gifts!
Zoey gets annoyed because our walk is getting interrupted but she puts up with the kids petting her, too. We are total opposites. Every time we go for a walk, she wants to chase every bunny and squirrel. I do, too, but I want to bring them home and play with them.

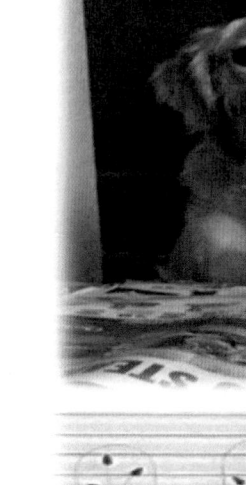

I have many friends. This is Winston, the escape artist. We all spend a lot of time chasing him.

Sadie is my super sweet friend. She is totally spoiled. She also thinks she is a person. Finally, this is my girlfriend, Liberty. She somehow knows when I am coming before I even get near there. She barks like crazy until someone opens the door and comes running out to see me. Isn't she cute?

When I think of what my life was like before, I think it is amazing how things can change in no time.

I learned some things that I think might help you too. I learned that sometimes the people who love you can hurt you. It's not your fault! If they keep hurting you, tell someone and make it stop. If you know of someone being hurt and they can't ask for help, do it for them. That includes animals because we can't get it for ourselves. Mom and Dad show me compassion every day. They don't get mad or hit me if I roll in the mud. They just give me another bath. Mom lets me help her in the garden and she still loves me even if I accidentally choose to lay there. They do a lot of little things to be kind. They know I struggle with steps so they made a ramp to help me get in and out of the house.

I also learned that not everyone is going to love you. Some people may not even like you. That is okay. You won't like everyone you meet either. You just have to find your people (or animals). There will always be someone who "gets" you and values you. That's who you should spend time with. Don't put a lot of energy into trying to please people who always want to find a reason to treat you badly. It won't change them. You are not the problem. Just be kind and treat people well and the people you want in your life will be there. Sometimes, all you need is one good friend. I found mine. They love me even with all my flaws. We all have very different personalities but we love and respect each other and we make it work.

My life was really bad for a while and I felt hopeless. Life is always changing and we never know what tomorrow will hold. If today is a bad day for you, please know that tomorrow is a new day. Sometimes good things can come from bad.
Challenges are for learning and they are only temporary obstacles. Break a bad mood by doing things that make you happy like walks, naps, lying in the sun or shade, enjoying a nice breeze, and back scratches. Spend even more time with people or animals who love you. Talk about it and let them help you through the bad times. Do something kind for someone. The quickest way to FEEL good is to DO good. You hold more power than you think.

Love, Grizzbear

Facts about Shelter Dogs

1. There are more homeless animals than people.
2. Adopting from a shelter is cheaper than a breeder.
3. Shelter dogs are perfectly normal.
4. Most dogs in the shelter are young.
5. Not all shelter dogs are mutts. There are many purebreds available.
6. Millions of dogs are sent to shelters every year.
7. Every shelter dog is carefully evaluated.
8. Dogs give children a better home environment.
9. Dogs teach love and compassion.
10. Dogs help children better cope with stress.
11. Sadly, only about 40% of shelter dogs find a forever home.
12. Overpopulation is a huge problem.
13. Most shelter dogs have already been fixed.
14. Many shelter dogs are already trained.
15. When you adopt, you are supporting a good cause.
16. Shelter dogs love people.
17. Owning a dog can help you live longer.

All animals deserve a loving home.

20

Happy to "Bee" Me - Once upon a time, there was a busy beehive. Everyone was busy doing their job except for a little worker bee. She didn't want to just be a worker bee. Hannah learns that everyone is important and needed. The book contains a story within a story and teaches children some rules of phonics as the letter P wants to be more important in her world.

Love, Bandit-A "tail" of foster care -Bandit is a lovable, sometimes mischievous raccoon who finds himself in foster care with complete strangers, new rules, and many confusing emotions. He eventually works his way through the emotional conflicts to find happiness and acceptance. The story is told from the perspective of the foster child. This book is a wonderful tool for introducing the feelings that accompany leaving a birth family, learning about rules and new environments, and learning to love and trust again. The book contains a list of famous people who were in foster care or adopted, and a "My Story" area where the child can write in his or her own story.

Love you, Teddy-A "tail" of loss and hope -Teddy is a young bear whose carefree, secure life is shattered when his father dies suddenly Teddy and his family struggle through the grief process. He is finally able to find a balance between the memories of the past and having happiness in the present The book includes a section for the child to write in "My Story".

I Love You Anyway-A "tail of understanding ADHD -Tagalong is a young raccoon who has ADHD. He always seems to be doing the wrong things at the wrong times and many times he isn't listening when his mother gives directions. His brothers enjoy teasing him about this very much. One day, easy going Tagalong has enough and runs away. Unfortunately, he forgets the dangers mom warned him about It is a close call and a learning experience for the whole family Tagalong learns the importance of paying attention and his family learns to have more patience and understanding. The book contains 40 reasons why it is good to have ADHD, famous people who have/had ADHD, and a section for children to write "My Story".

BullyFish -Once upon a time, in a peaceful aquarium, lived a happy community of sea critters. They had their problems but they always worked things out until the bully moved in. The bully took over their lives and their tank. This group of friends must figure out how to solve their problem so they can live happily again The book contains tips for kids and a list of famous people who were bullied and advice they have shared.

To order these books visit H2HResources.com or Heart 2 Heart Resources on Facebook
Several of our books are YouTube videos. Look for the Heart 2 Heart Resources page!

21

Made in the USA
Lexington, KY
04 December 2019